THE FISHERMAN AND THE BIRD

by Sonia Levitin
illustrated by
Francis Livingston

Parnassus Press Oakland California
Houghton Mifflin Company Boston 1982

JP

A PARNASSUS PRESS BOOK

H 10 9 8 7 6 5 4 3 2 1

Library of Congress Cataloging in Publication Data
Levitin, Sonia, 1934-
      The fisherman and the bird.

      Summary: A reclusive fisherman's neighbors try
to persuade him not to harm the rare birds that
have nested in his boat.
      [1. Rare birds—Fiction.   2. Friendship—Fiction]
I. Livingston, Francis, ill.   II. Title.
PZ7.L58Fi   [E]   81-18840
ISBN 0-395-31860-2   AACR2

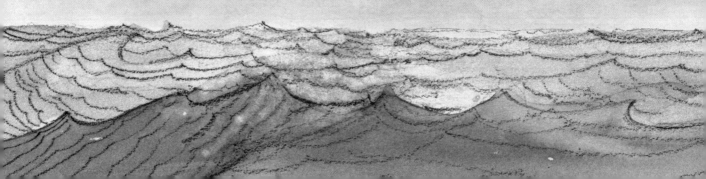

To John Larrecq
with gratitude for the beauty he created
in his work

In a lovely little fishing village lived Rico, the fisherman, all alone in his hut. It was rumored that in his youth Rico had loved one of the village girls, but that she had left him for another. Since then he stayed away from other people, rising early to catch fish in his large nets, then going home to a solitary supper. Thus, twenty years had passed, and now he was no longer young.

In the past the other fishermen used to invite Rico to join them at the tavern, or to come to church with them on Sundays. Rico always refused, saying, "People are foolish and false. I'd rather sit alone and sing to the fishes."

Nobody ever heard Rico singing in the village. But when he had sailed his boat to some quiet inlet, Rico would throw back his head and sing until the loneliness left his heart.

Early one morning when Rico went to his boat, he sensed something strange. Even in the dim light his keen eyes saw everything. His boat swayed on the black water as always. His ropes were coiled neatly upon the deck, his nets ready for the day's fishing. But some strange presence made Rico pause. He heard a fluttering. He saw the flash of white feathers. High on the mast of Rico's boat a large brown and white bird was building a nest.

Carefully Rico stepped onto his boat. The bird pushed a twig into the nest. Now, in the early light, Rico could see the soft upper feathers, like a gleaming cape of brown and bronze. What a beautiful creature, he thought, and for a long moment the bird fixed its bright golden eye on Rico.

"Bird, get off my boat," Rico said gruffly. "I must go to net my fish."

As if it understood, the bird flew away, disappearing over the water. Rico set out for his day's work.

No sooner had he come to his favorite inlet, when the
bird reappeared. It circled slowly, then landed on the mast
of Rico's boat. In its beak it held a long piece of string,
which it added carefully to the nest.

Rico began to sing in a loud voice, hoping to frighten the bird away. The bird was startled. It rose with a fearful screech. But as Rico continued to sing the bird glided down to the mast and remained there, listening.

Rico sang out with angry gestures, his arms flung wide. The bird cocked its head.

Rico shouted, "You cannot stay here!" He swung his cap and shook his fist. "No fish will come near my nets when

they see you above the water! Everyone knows that birds
like you eat fish."

Still the bird stayed, its wings folded, listening.

"Be gone! Scat! What sort of fool do you think I am that
I would let you build your nest on my mast?"

The bird flew away to a tiny island. Soon it returned with
a beakful of twigs. It formed them to the nest, which was
growing round and large.

"When I get back to shore," Rico warned, "I will get a
long pole and push that nest of yours off into the water."

All morning Rico threatened the bird. All morning the bird continued to build the nest. Later that day, when Rico sailed into the harbor, there atop the mast sat the shining bird in its nest.

The other fishermen stopped and pointed. They laughed and laughed. "Rico, you have taken a strange creature for

a friend. It will surely frighten the fish away. Let's see what you caught in your nets today," they teased.

Rico was ashamed to show his catch, it was so small.

"You'd better get rid of that bird," they called, "or it will be trouble for you!"

"That is exactly what I'll do," shouted Rico, steering his boat toward the dock.

A crowd had gathered. Women coming to meet their husbands' boats and children on the way home from school all stopped and stared at the strange sight of the large bird nesting on the mast.

Angrily Rico picked up a long pole that lay on the dock. What right had these people to laugh at him, or tell him what to do? He was the master of this boat. He would not allow that bird to stay and make a fool of him.

"Don't break the nest," the women cried. "Let us try to move it gently onto the pilings."

The children jumped up and down, flapping their arms as though they were wings. They called to the bird, "Ca-caa!" but still the bird remained motionless.

Rico held the pole high over his head. He raised himself on his toes. He was about to strike when he heard a shout from the dock.

"Wait! Wait, old man! Do not strike that bird."

Rico spun around, furious. Old man! Who dared to call him old? Who dared to shout at him?

In the next moment Rico's boat dipped as someone jumped aboard. It was the village teacher, a serious young man dressed in dark garments.

"Get off my boat, Teacher," Rico said scornfully, "lest you soil your fancy clothes."

"Please, please wait," the teacher begged. "You'll have time enough to destroy that nest, only listen before you decide."

"Speak then," said Rico harshly as he set down the pole, "and be quick."

"That bird," said the teacher breathlessly, "is very rare. Only a few like it have been seen near here for years and years. Many have died on other shores by eating fish from unclean waters, and thoughtless people have destroyed their nesting places."

"It looks like an ordinary bird to me," grumbled Rico. "Maybe you lie."

"Come to the schoolhouse then!" cried the teacher. "There I have great books. You will see for yourself a picture of this bird. It is a rare creature. Sometimes rare animals and birds even become extinct."

Rico scoffed. "I do not know what that means – extinct. Teacher, you mock me. I am a poor fisherman. You use large words to confuse me."

"Extinct," said the teacher, "means to die, not only one creature or a few, but the whole group." The teacher sighed. "It means no babies will ever hatch again. Then, all birds of this kind would be gone from the earth forever."

Rico looked up at the bird, gazing at its beautiful out-stretched wings as it now flew away to a tree.

"It is seeking its mate," the teacher explained. "The mate also searches for twigs and moss to build the nest. Now, if we are careful not to frighten them, the birds will hatch their eggs here, and soon others will follow. These beautiful birds will be saved."

"You mean they will always make nests on our boats?" Rico exclaimed.

"No," said the teacher. "I will ask the children to help me make nesting platforms for them. But if you move this nest now, the smell of your hands will be upon it. The birds will not return. All will be lost."

On the dock the crowd stood silently. In Rico's chest was a heavy thumping he had not felt in many years. He glanced up at the sky.

True to the teacher's word, another, even larger, bird returned with the first carrying moss to the nest. In gliding circles they flew together, their dark-tipped wings throwing bold shadows across Rico and the crowd. Then, suddenly, together they landed on the rail of Rico's boat.

Rico pushed the teacher aside. "I must go now and bring in my catch," he said. "The birds may stay here for tonight. In the morning — we will see."

Confused, angry, and extremely tired, Rico returned to his hut. He felt too weak even to prepare his poor supper. He closed his eyes, and in the darkness came the vision of the large birds etched against the sky. All night they drifted through his thoughts and guided his dreams. He awakened just as tired as when he lay down.

As he walked toward the dock, Rico clenched his fists and made a decision. Now, while it was still dark, he would break that nest to pieces. What, after all, did he owe that creature? Nothing. It had stolen his catch. It had taken his strength. It had made him look foolish in front of the other fishermen.

All these years he had kept away from people with their falseness and foolishness, only to be mocked by this bird. He would not allow it. He would stand firm.

A single word crept through his mind. "Extinct." Rico shrugged it off. He would not be so weak as to let a mere bird take over his boat, ruin his life, make him a laughing-stock.

Thus, when Rico arrived at the dock he immediately seized the long pole, took it to his boat and lifted it high over his head.

At this moment he heard a crooning, gentle sound.

Rico looked up. There on the mast sat the mother bird, its body tucked deep into the nest, while the mate circled round and round. Both birds crooned softly, sweetly, as if they were singing a song of love.

For a long time Rico stood motionless, the pole clutched in his hands. As daylight appeared, both birds suddenly flew down to the rail, and when the other fishermen arrived they saw Rico gazing at the two large birds, scratching his head.

"Rico!" they called, laughing. "Are you having a conversation with your friends? Are you solving all the problems of the world together?"

The children had run down to the docks before school. They hopped up and down, flapping their arms, squealing with excitement.

Rico faced the crowd, shouting, "I am climbing up to see exactly what those birds have put inside the nest. It is my right. This is, after all, my boat."

Thereupon Rico climbed up the rigging, bent over, and peered into the nest.

"What do you see, Rico?" called the fishermen, swinging their caps, laughing rudely. "Did they perhaps leave you a few gold pieces in there?"

"What in the world does he expect to find?" cried the women who had come, too. "Is he looking for elves in there?"

The children giggled and pointed until the teacher came and silenced them. He called up to Rico in calm, respectful tones, "What do you see there, fisherman? Tell us, does something lie in that nest?"

Rico turned, looked down and nodded. "Eggs," he said so softly that his words were almost lost. "There are two eggs in the nest."

He came down the rigging. As he did so the mother bird flew back and settled herself upon the nest, while the mate again circled in the sky.

"Tell us about the eggs," asked the teacher, his eyes shining.

"They are larger than the eggs of a hen," Rico said. "They are spotted, and the color of pale gold, like the shore when the sun is setting."

The other fishermen held their caps in their hands, grinning shyly. They looked at Rico in a different way.

The women sighed and smiled mysteriously.

The children wriggled with delight, struggling to keep quiet, for the teacher stood soberly by, his face gleaming with pride.

"At last," he said, "it is accomplished. And the mother bird, you see, is faithful as is the father. Soon the eggs will hatch." He turned to the crowd. "We will all celebrate the

great moment together."

"That may be good for you," Rico grumbled. "I still must make a living." He bent to pull in the rope that held his boat tied to the dock, but the teacher cried out.

"Wait! You cannot move this boat. It will frighten the birds! They will leave the nest, and the eggs will never hatch. Please, I beg you, do not move the boat!"

Rico was stunned. It was one thing to allow the bird and the nest to remain on his mast; it was quite another to sit idly on the docks. A fisherman must go to sea.

Sternly he asked the teacher, "How long will it take the eggs to hatch?"

"I think thirty-three days," the teacher replied.

"Teacher, you are crazy," Rico said. "If I do not fish I will starve."

The teacher turned to the crowd, his hands outstretched for help.

"Leave the bird alone, Rico," the other fishermen called. "We will share our catch with you. Do not worry so for your mouthful of food."

The women joined the outcry. "You have worked too long without a rest, Rico. Stay here in the village. Sit on the dock. We will be happy to hear you sing to us as you sing to the fishes!"

And the children shouted, "Oh, please, Rico, let the little birds hatch, and we will sing and dance for happiness."

Wordlessly Rico nodded.

Day after day Rico sat on the dock holding the long pole in his hands to frighten away any birds which might try to harm the bird in the nest.

As he sat, Rico sang to himself. He watched the villagers going about their tasks. Soon he called them all by name. Sometimes the women brought him freshly baked bread, and the children came to tell him stories.

So day followed day after day, until the last, the most important day dawned. That morning Rico hurried to the dock, his heart quickening with excitement. Today! Today!

But as he waited hour after hour, Rico's excitement turned to dread. What if something went wrong? What if the eggs failed to hatch? What if the little chicks inside were already dead?

Rico grieved, his head bent low. He had felt this way once before, long ago. The pain of disappointment seemed too great to bear.

Then, at mid-afternoon, suddenly Rico heard a new sound. Oh! Oh! He heard a pecking, a crackling, and the flapping and squawking of the mother bird, praising and urging her little ones to break free of the eggs and to live.

Rico stood for a moment dumbfounded. Then he flung down the pole and began to run.

He ran up the narrow, crooked street to the church, where he beat upon the tower door until it was flung open.

"Ring the bell!" Rico panted to the astonished priest.

"Have you news to proclaim?"

"Indeed!"

"Then you may ring the bell yourself," said the priest.

Rico climbed up the winding stair, grasped the long rope and pulled with all his might, until the bell rang out over the village. It called the women in their houses, the school children and their teacher, the village tradesmen, and even the fishermen in their boats. Everyone ran to gather at the church, while the bell rang and rang.

At last Rico went to the tower window. He looked down at all the people, and with his arms outspread he shouted joyously, "Arrived!"

Overcome with happiness, Rico began to sing in a voice so strong that it echoed from the distant hills.

ARRIVED! ARRIVED! ARRIVED!

THE LITTLE BIRDS HAVE ARRIVED, AND ALL IS WELL!

The people joined hands, laughing, dancing and singing with Rico, "All is well! All is well! All is well!"